The Dog That Stole Home

Other books in this series

MATT CHRISTOPHER
The Dog That Stole Home

Illustrated by Daniel Vasconcellos

 Little, Brown and Company

Boston   New York   Toronto   London

First Paperback Edition

Library of Congress Cataloging-in-Publication Data

Christopher, Matt.
    The dog that stole home / Matt Christopher ; illustrated by Daniel Vasconcellos. — 1st ed.
        p.   cm.
    Summary: When his telepathic dog Harry is grounded for nipping another dog, Mike wonders how he'll ever make it through the baseball game without his advice and encouragement. Sequel to "The Dog That Pitched a No-Hitter."
    ISBN 0-316-14082-1 (hc)
    ISBN 0-316-14187-9 (pb)

    [1. Dogs — Fiction.   2. Extrasensory perception — Fiction.   3. Baseball — Fiction.]   I. Vasconcellos, Daniel, ill.   II. Title.
PZ7.C458Dp   1993
[E] — dc20   92-15613

                10 9 8 7 6 5 4 3 2   (hc)
                10 9 8 7 6 5 4 3 2   (pb)

                            BP

            Published simultaneously in Canada
        by Little, Brown & Company (Canada) Limited

        Printed in the United States of America

To Timmy and Tommy Oertel — M.C.

To my parents, Dolores and Arthur — D.V.

Harry chased after the tennis ball, leaped up two feet into the air, and caught it in his mouth. Head held high, he trotted back to Mike and dropped the ball at his feet. "Wuff!" he barked as he ran back down the street to wait for the next throw.

"Great catch, Harry!" Mike praised him. "Maybe I can talk Coach Wilson into putting you in our outfield!"

"Sure! And maybe I'll get my picture in the paper!" Harry replied. He posed as if the cameras were already snapping.

Even though he was a fuzzy Airedale, Harry was able to communicate with Mike through

extrasensory perception — ESP. Mike and Harry had read each other's thoughts for the first time in the pet shop. Of course, Mike had bought Harry right away.

Now, as he wound up to throw the ball again, Mike wondered what he would ever do without Harry.

"Well, for one thing, you'd still be pitching instead of using that great throwing arm at second base," Harry replied.

Mike laughed as he hurled the ball down the street. Sometimes he forgot Harry knew everything he was thinking.

The ball arced higher and farther than before. Again Harry caught it, but instead of bringing it back he danced around just out of Mike's reach.

"Can't catch me!" he teased. Mike could tell Harry was grinning even though he had the tennis ball in his mouth.

Mike groaned. He knew from previous experience that he'd have to chase and tag Harry before he'd get the ball back. He took a deep breath and charged down the street, legs pumping.

Mike was just about to touch Harry's fur when out of nowhere a tan-and-white dog twice the size of Harry broke away from a girl and joined in the race. Harry was so surprised he dropped the ball. The big dog snatched it up and took off.

"Hey! Come back with that!" Mike yelled.

"Sam!" shouted the big dog's owner. "Bring that back!" Harry was after Sam like a shot.

"Don't worry, Mike!" Harry's thoughts swept back to Mike. "I've got it covered!"

I'll say, thought Mike as he slowed to a walk. That dog is faster than the speed of sound!

"Thanks, ol' boy," Harry panted.

In a matter of seconds Harry caught up with the thief. He tried to wrestle the tennis ball from Sam's mouth, but the big dog just wouldn't let go. He whipped his head from side to side, growling menacingly.

But Harry wouldn't scare. Instead, he nipped Sam lightly on the nose.

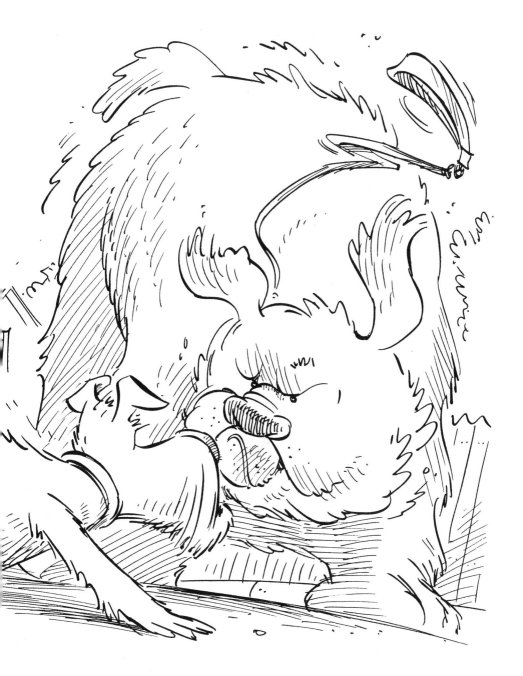

With a loud *yelp!*, Sam dropped the ball.
Harry scooped it up and trotted back to Mike.

The big dog was still yelping.

"That animal of yours should be fenced in!
It's dangerous!" cried the girl as she rushed
past Mike. "Sam! Oh, my poor little Sam!"

8

"Little?" Harry echoed. "I barely touched the big lunk. Besides, he ruined a good race!"

"Lucky for you he did, too!" Mike chuckled. "I was *this* close to beating you! That would've wiped that grin off your face, I'll bet!"

Harry stood up on his hind legs, put his fore-paws over his eyes, and whined pitifully. Mike snorted, then turned to see the girl and her dog continue their walk as if nothing had happened.

"Michael! Come here! And bring that dog with you!"

Mike whirled to see his mother standing on the front porch of their house. From the look on her face, he knew that he and Harry were in big trouble.

"Okay, Mom!" he said.

Mike and Harry went to the house.

"Mike, I saw Harry snap at that dog," his mother said. "I know he's not vicious, but I'm worried that he might try to nip someone at your game tomorrow. I'm afraid Harry will have to stay home until he learns not to bite."

"But we're playing the number one team tomorrow! If we beat them, we'll have a chance at the playoffs. You know I always play better when Harry's there," Mike cried.

"Well, you'll just have to play without him there tomorrow. Please put him in the backyard and teach him to behave," his mother said. She turned and went back into the house.

"Grounded," Harry huffed. "I might as well be put into solitary confinement." He looked up at Mike's worried face. "Sorry, pal. Guess I should have let the big bully have the ball."

Mike sighed as he opened the gate to the backyard. What was he going to do without Harry's support tomorrow?

15

The game against the Robin Hood Arrows
started at four o'clock the next day. The Arrows
were up first. Mike, playing second base, kept
glancing at the spot by the Giants' dugout
where Harry usually lay. The spot looked very
empty.

The Arrows got off to a flying start. The lead-
off batter, Robbie McAllister, laced a double.

16

Then the Giants' pitcher gave up a walk and a single to put the Arrows on the scoreboard before the first out was made. A blooping fly over second base — just over Mike's head — added a second run to the first.

Rats! thought Mike. I bet I would have had that one if Harry'd been here. He pounded his fist into his glove.

The next Arrow batter struck out, but another double put them up to three runs before a fly ball ended the first half of the inning.

The Giants came to bat, and it was one, two, three. Just like that.

The Arrows batted again, and again the lead-off batter belted a solid double. The Giants' pitcher, Omar Petri, looked a little shaken and gave up two walks in a row. Arrows 4, Giants 0.

Mike heard the first baseman grumble. At least I had Harry's support when I played pitcher, Mike thought.

Out loud, he yelled, "C'mon Omar! Strike out this next guy!"

As if Mike's words had given him just the help he'd needed, Omar fired three sizzlers in

18

a row for the first out. Two fly balls added the last two outs, and the Giants were back up to bat.

Omar led off with a double to right field. While Mike warmed up on deck, the second batter, Monk Solomon, took four balls for a walk.

Now's my chance to make up for that missed catch, Mike thought as he approached the plate.

The first pitch came in just at waist level, and Mike swung hard. A solid hit down the first base line! Dropping the bat, Mike took off. The Arrows' first baseman, Jim Morrow, rushed forward and scooped up the ball. Mike put on a burst of speed, but Jim beat him to the bag. Mike was out.

A strikeout and a pop-up ended the inning.

The Arrows could do nothing in the third. But the Giants, at their turn at bat, made a turnaround and came up with two runs.

The fourth and fifth innings went scoreless for both teams.

The Arrows didn't add to their 4–2 lead in the top of the sixth, either. The Giants, on the other hand, earned two runs to tie up the game before the inning ended.

That's more like it! Mike thought excitedly. Too bad you're missing this one, Harry. It's a humdinger.

As Mike got his glove and ran onto the field, a familiar voice entered his mind.

"It sure is," it said.

Mike's heart jumped. There, in his usual spot, tail snapping back and forth, was Harry!

"Hey! How'd you get here?" Mike cried.

Harry grinned. "You'll never guess," he said
and pointed his nose toward the stands.

Mike glanced up and saw his mother watch-
ing him with a smile.

A call from a teammate reminded Mike the inning was about to start. "What changed her mind?" he asked Harry as he ran toward second base.

"I'll explain later. Just get out there and play some heads-up ball!" replied Harry.

The Arrows threatened to break the 4–4 tie at the top of the seventh. Their first batter nailed a single and Omar walked the second. A fly out held the two runners at first and second, but then the Arrows' strongest batter, Robbie McAllister, came to bat.

"Get ready, pal," Harry said. "He looks like he means business!"

Mike crouched down low. Omar studied the batter for a second and then fired.

Crack!

Robbie connected for a line drive that just missed the top of Omar's glove. The Giants' shortstop, Rich Gates, snared it and snapped it to Mike at second, and then Mike relayed it to first.

A double play!

"Okay!" cried Coach Wilson, clapping like crazy. "Let's do it! Let's break the tie!"

Mike realized he was the third man up. Heart pounding, he watched Omar fly out, then the second batter, Monk Solomon, swish at three pitches.

"Belt it, Mike," said Harry calmly. "A home run will do it, you know."

"Sure," said Mike as he stepped to the plate. "It's easy enough from the sidelines!" He gripped the bat and waited for the first pitch.

Crack! He laced the pitcher's first throw to deep right center field. The crowd cheered as he bolted around the bases. For a moment he thought he'd hit a homer, but Coach Wilson held him to a triple.

"Attaboy, Mike!" said the coach, slapping him on the shoulder. "A little more speed and you might have made it home!"

Rich Gates was up next. He'd struck out his last time at bat. There was no telling what would happen now.

"Mike, listen," Harry's voice entered his head.

"Yeah?" Mike answered, concentrating on the pitcher.

"Here's your chance to score," Harry said. "Listen to me, and listen closely."

Harry got up and walked over to third base. He stopped just behind Mike.

"You're going to steal," Harry said.

Mike stared down at Harry.

"Steal? I can't!" he cried. "Not in Little League!"

"You can . . . when the pitcher doesn't have the ball," growled the Airedale. "Now get ready! When I give the signal, give it all you've got!"

"You've lost your marbles! I'm not fast enough to beat the ball!" Nevertheless, he crouched with his hands on his knees. Heart racing, he waited for the next pitch. I don't know who's crazier, me or that dog, he thought.

"We'll talk about that later," Harry chuckled. "Get ready!"

The Arrows' pitcher stepped onto the mound, glanced at Mike, then turned his attention to Rich.

"Ball!" boomed the ump.

Then, just as the Arrows' catcher was in the act of tossing the ball back to the pitcher, Harry yelled: "Catch me!"

Then he took off, bolting toward home. A split second later, Mike was after him. It had never been so important for him to tag Harry!

Mike was halfway to home plate when the Giants' fans began to shout, "Go, Mike, go! Faster! Faster!" His mother's voice rang above the rest.

He was within five feet of the plate when he saw the Arrows' catcher covering the plate, his mitt ready for the catch.

"Hit it!" yelled Harry.

Mike did. His hand touched home plate just as the catcher reached up for the ball. There was an endless moment of silence before the umpire called the play.

"Safe!"

The crowd exploded into one of the loudest roars Mike had ever heard. Grinning, he stood up and brushed the dirt off his uniform as his teammates swarmed around him.

"Unbelievable!" cried Omar, slapping him on

the back. "I've never seen anyone run so fast."

"I'm surprised you didn't trip over your dog," Coach Wilson said, smiling. "It almost looked like he was daring you to beat him."

Mike looked down at Harry, who grinned and winked.

The two teams shook hands and then headed to their dugouts.

"How'd you get out, anyway? That's what I'd like to know," Mike asked Harry as he picked up his glove.

"Well . . . ," Harry chuckled.

Mike turned to see his mother approaching.

"Mike, that was amazing," she said, ruffling Harry's fur.

"Thanks, Mom. And thanks for bringing Harry!"

"Well, I didn't have much choice. I'd never seen Harry look so depressed," she said.

"Depressed?" echoed Mike. Harry stood up on his hind legs, put his forepaws over his eyes, and whined like he'd lost his best friend.

"See?" cried his mother, throwing up her hands.

Mike burst out laughing.

"You're crazy, you know that?" he snorted.

Harry moved one paw and peered up at Mike.

"Yes," replied Harry, "but lovable, too, right?"

Mike laughed again and scooped Harry in his arms. "You bet," he whispered.

42